LUCY MAUD MONTGOMERY BIRTHPLACE
NEW LONDON
PRINCE EDWARD ISLAND

Based on the Sullivan Films production
"Road to Avonlea"™
with selected quotations from the books:
*The Story Girl, The Golden Road,
Chronicles of Avonlea,* and
Further Chronicles of Avonlea
by Lucy Maud Montgomery

THE
Avonlea
ALBUM

Edited by Fiona McHugh

A FIREFLY BOOK

A FIREFLY BOOK

Editor: Fiona McHugh
Design: Michael Solomon

Cinematography: Peter Luxford
            Reginald Morris
            Manfred Guthe

Still photography by: Michaelin McDermott
            C. Stewart Brady

Photographs on pages 56–57, 60, 64–65, 71:
            Barrett and MacKay,
            Masterfile

Firefly Books Ltd.
250 Sparks Ave.,
Willowdale, Ontario
M2H 2S4

Canadian Cataloguing in Publication Data

Main entry under title:

The Avonlea album

Includes writings of L.M. Montgomery.
ISBN 0-920668-96-8 (bound)   ISBN 0-920668-97-6 (pbk.)

1. Road to Avonlea (Television program) — Juvenile
literature. 2. Television actors and actresses —
Canada — Portraits — Juvenile literature.
I. Montgomery, L.M. (Lucy Maud), 1874–1942.

PN1992.77.R63A86 1991   j791.45'72   C91-094438-5

Printed and bound in Canada

PREFACE

Summer had ended in 1910 when Lucy Maud Montgomery laid down her pen with genuine regret. She had just finished writing her fourth book, *The Story Girl*. Sitting at her table by the window in her "dear white room," the author mentally bade farewell to her characters and, in a sense, to her youth.

Montgomery sensed that *The Story Girl* would be the last book she would ever write in her home in Cavendish, Prince Edward Island, where she had dreamt, suffered and grown up. That home was owned by her ailing grandmother and would pass, on her grandmother's death, to an uncle who lived nearby. As inexorably as her grandmother's life neared its end, Montgomery's time on her beloved Island was drawing to a close.

This sense of love and longing for times past pervades *The Story Girl*, which remained Montgomery's favourite amongst the many books she would go on to write. "An idyll of childhood on an old P. E. Island farm," was how she once described it. At 35, with her own childhood long since past, Montgomery knew that her life stood on the verge of major change. For the past four years she had been engaged to the Reverend Ewan Macdonald, the man she would finally marry in 1911, four months after the death of her grandmother.

Two years later, having moved to Leaskdale, Ontario, and borne her first child, Montgomery wrote a sequel to *The Story Girl*. She called it *The Golden Road*, and in it she returned to Prince Edward Island and to the childhood she held preserved in the amber light of memory.

These two books, *The Story Girl* and *The Golden Road* form the framework of the family television series, *The Road to Avonlea*. Additional characters and incidents from two collections of Montgomery's short stories, *Chronicles of Avonlea* and *Further Chronicles of Avonlea*, lend texture and density to the structure. Thematically and visually, *The Road to Avonlea* strives to recreate Lucy Maud Montgomery's dream of childhood, that "fair, lost" place "with a spell of eternity woven over it."

Passages in italics have been drawn from the following works by L.M. Montgomery: *The Story Girl; The Golden Road; Chronicles of Avonlea; Further Chronicles of Avonlea.*

PROLOGUE

WHEN Sara Stanley first set reluctant foot on the *Road to Avonlea*, she little dreamt what treasure she might find at the end of it.

Sara had grown up in the city of Montreal, the only daughter of a wealthy widower, whose wife had died shortly after Sara's birth.

At first glance, Sara's life might have seemed ideal. Her father adored and spoiled her. She had pretty dresses galore, the best of food and play-things, and servants at her beck and call. Instead of going to school she took lessons at home from her Nanny. In short, she was surrounded by all the luxury a wealthy father could bestow on his motherless child.

A closer look might have revealed that everything was not quite as it should be in Sara's life. In her inner-most heart, she grieved over her mother's absence. The early death of her mother had not only deprived Sara of her company, but it also made her feel singled out, set apart from other children who had real-life mothers to cling to and bicker with and love.

Then too, Sara missed her father. As a successful business man, Blair Stanley travelled constantly. Sara was often left alone for weeks on end, with no-one to talk to but the elderly Nanny Banks. Sometimes she longed for the companionship of someone her own age, a brother or a sister, in whom she might confide. When these blue-tinged moods overtook her, Sara would seek refuge in books. Books became for her a source of comfort and inspiration. With their help, she began to develop her own story-telling gifts. "I may not have a friend," she would think to herself. "But at least I have an imagination. And a fertile imagination can be the best of company."

Then one day, without warning, Sara's privileged world collapses. Her father is arrested and charged with embezzlement. The victim of an unscrupulous business partner, Blair Stanley determines to fight the charges and clear his name. In the meantime, Sara must be sent out of the city, away from the gossip and rumours his misfortune will create. But where? Casting about for

somewhere remote yet accessible, Blair finally settles on Avonlea.

Ruth Stanley, Sara's mother, grew up in Avonlea, a tiny village on the shores of Prince Edward Island. Her name in those days was Ruth King and many of her relatives still live on the Island. Although he has not spoken to any of the King clan since Ruth's death, Blair feels confident that they will provide Sara with a good home.

It all happens quickly, too quickly for Sara's taste. Before she can open her mouth to protest, she is packed off with Nanny Banks to stay with relatives she never knew she possessed, in a place she never knew existed. To her, the road to Avonlea seems like the long, bleak road into exile.

And at first the quiet, tree-hushed village, with its red dirt roads, its snug farmsteads and its one-room school house, seems to Sara a dire form of punishment indeed.

Only gradually, as she draws closer to her King cousins and aunts and uncle, does it dawn on the lonely, bookish girl that in Avonlea she has found treasure beyond compare. In Avonlea she has found warmth and companionship and love. She has found, in short, her family.

This album represents a pictorial record of Sara's first year in Avonlea. In time to come, when she has grown up and put away childish things forever, she will turn these pages and find herself back once again on that golden road of childhood, whose memories remain "the dearest of our eternal possessions."

Montreal ...

Sara's heart felt heavy as lead. She knew her
father was in trouble. Yet instead of being able
to comfort him, she was being bundled off with
Nanny Banks to stay with relatives she barely
knew.

As the carriage trundled by the orchard that late Spring evening, Sara lifted her bent head. The beauty of the unfamiliar world around her seemed to clamour for attention.

There were so many delights along the golden road to give us pleasure-the earth dappled with new blossom, the dance of shadows in the fields, the rustling, rain-wet ways of the woods, the faint fragrance in meadow lanes, liltings of birds and croon of bees in the old orchard, windy pipings on the hills, sunset behind the pines ...

"It's like a dream of fairyland — as if you were walking in a king's palace."

She lingered to lay a bunch of wild violets, misty blue and faintly sweet, on her mother's grave.

Ruth Stanley
1871 – 1894

King Farm

Off to the right was a dim, branching place which we knew was the orchard; and on our left, among sibilant spruces and firs, was the old ... house.

Sara's cousins: Felix (11), Felicity (13) and Cecily (9) King.

Sara's Aunt Janet and Uncle Alec King.

Aunt Janet, a big, bustling, sonsy woman, with full-blown peony cheeks ... gave us so much good advice and was so constantly telling us to do this or not to do the other thing, that we could not remember half her instructions, and did not try.

•

To Uncle Alec we gave our warmest love. We felt that we always had a friend at court in Uncle Alec no matter what we did or left undone.

•

To be sure, Felicity was a stunning beauty. But, with the swift and unerring intuition of childhood, which feels in a moment what it sometimes takes maturity much time to perceive, we realised that she was rather too well aware of her good looks. In brief, we saw that Felicity was vain.

Rose Cottage, home of Hetty and Olivia King, Sara's two unmarried aunts.

Behind the house was a grove of fir and spruce, a dim, cool place where the winds were fond of purring and where there was always a resinous, woodsy odour.

Since another cousin, Andrew King, was staying at King farm, Hetty and Olivia took Sara to live with them at Rose Cottage.

It was a time of wonder and marvel, of the soft touch of silver rain on greening fields, of the incredible delicacy of young leaves, of blossom in field and garden and wood. The whole world bloomed in a flush and tremor of ... loveliness.

The apple tree ... was a sight to see — a great tree-pyramid with high, far-spreading boughs, over which a wealth of rosy snow seemed to have been flung.

Aunt Hetty, Avonlea schoolmistress, and the eldest of the King clan.

She was one of those people who always speak decisively. If they merely announce that they are going to peel the potatoes for dinner, their hearers realize that there is no possible escape for the potatoes.

She was dark, with a rich dusky sort of darkness, suggestive of the bloom on purple plums, or the glow of deep red apples among bronze leaves.

Olivia King, Sara's youngest aunt.

"Aunt Olivia spoils you," said Felicity.
"She doesn't either, Felicity King! Aunt Olivia is just sweet. She kisses me good-night every night, and your mother never kisses you."
"My mother doesn't make kisses so common," retorted Felicity.
"But she gives us pie for dinner every day."

The village of Avonlea, with its verdant,
tree-lined streets and sleepy rhythms, reminded
Sara of a place from a bygone tale.

*After the rain the air seemed dripping with odours
in the warm west wind — the tang of fir balsam, the
spice of mint, the wild woodsiness of ferns, the aroma
of grasses steeping in the sunshine, — and with it all
a breath of wild sweetness from far hill pastures.*

At first the children held aloof from Sara. To them she seemed an exotic bird, flaunting its feathers on their small pond.

•

Andrew, the son of Uncle Roger King, had been sent to live in Avonlea while his father led a geological expedition to Brazil.

By the time she had lived for a fortnight in Avonlea, Sara was beginning to feel as if she might, someday, belong. She was getting along better with her cousins too, in spite of some minor differences of opinion, mostly with Felicity ...

"It's so nice to be alive in the spring," said the Story Girl one twilight ...
"It's nice to be alive any time," said Felicity complacently.
"But it's nicer in the spring," insisted the Story Girl. "When I'm dead I think I'll feel dead all the rest of the year, but when spring comes I'm sure I'll feel like getting up and being alive again."

... it was evening before we were all free to meet in the orchard and loll on the grasses ... it was a place of shady sweetness, fragrant with the odour of ripening apples, full of dear, delicate shadows. Through its openings we looked afar to the blue rims of the hills and over green, old, tranquil fields, lying in the sunset glow. Overhead the lacing leaves made a green, murmurous roof. There was no such thing as hurry in the world, while we lingered there and talked of "cabbages and kings."

... they walked through the lane where lissome boughs of young saplings flicked against their heads, and the air was wildly sweet with the woodsy odours.

"It's star time and good-night time ..."

*Only in the country can one become truly acquainted
with the night. There it has the solemn calm of the
infinite. The dim, wide fields lie in silence, wrapped
in the holy mystery of darkness. A wind, loosened
from wild places far away, steals out to blow over
dewy, star-lit, immemorial hills. The air in the pastures is sweet with the hush of dreams, and one may
rest here like a child on its mother's breast.*

As the clear Spring days warmed into summer, Sara delighted in the carefree companionship of other children.

Sara's social horizons expanded too. She met Marilla Cuthbert, who lived at Green Gables ...

... and the formidable Mrs Rachel Lynde, who had come to live at Green Gables after Anne Shirley's departure.

She looked like a woman whose opinions were always very decided and warranted to wear.

She attended tea parties ...

... and cricket matches

... a laugh which put the mettle of her festal silk seams to the test.

Sara met Avonlea's eccentrics too ...

Alexander Abraham

"No woman has ever been known to get inside of his house since his sister died twenty years ago."

Old Lady Lloyd

Old Lady Lloyd was very proud, so proud that she would have died rather than let ... people ... suspect how poor she was.

Peg Bowen

"Peter Craig says she is a witch and that he bets she's at the bottom of it when the butter won't come. But I don't believe that. Witches are so scarce nowadays ... it's not likely there are any here right in Prince Edward Island."

That was also the summer Felicity first fell in love ...

His name was David and he barely noticed
Felicity, being more interested in conquering
the cricket field.

It was Gus Pike who helped Felicity put her feelings in perspective. A tall youth, with a winning way with a fiddle, there was an indefinable air of mystery about Gus, as though a secret hovered over him.

In that ... music was the joy of innocent, mirthful childhood, blent with the laughter of waves and the call of glad winds.

In August came a day of gold and blue ...

Each simple task helped Sara feel more at home. As she settled in, she began to observe some of the real-life stories around her.

•

There was Aunt Olivia's attachment to Jasper Dale, for instance, a shy, inventive genius. In Aunt Hetty's opinion, a King had no business falling for someone commonly referred to as the Awkward Man.

"You are unlike other people," she said softly, *"and that is why I love you."*

"He has such a nice face, even if he is awkward. He looks like a man you could tell things to."

"Well, I'd like a man who could move around without falling over his own feet," said Felicity.

"I wonder if it is true that he writes poetry," said the Story Girl. "Mrs Griggs says it is. She says she has seen him writing it in a brown book. She said she couldn't get near enough to read it, but she knew it was poetry by the shape of it."

"Very likely … I'd believe anything of him," said Felicity.

With Jasper Dale's help, Sara held a magic lantern show to raise money for the school library. That was the night she truly earned the name, by which the children had been calling her since her arrival in Avonlea: "the Story Girl."

Here was a performer who could be depended on ...
... the ... magic of her voice caught and held her listeners
spellbound.

Gazing dreamily afar ... she began, her voice giving to the words
and fancies of the old tale the delicacy of hoar frost and the crystal
sparkle of dew.

As for Aunt Hetty, she too had had her share
of romance ...

Many years ago, Romney Penhallow and Hetty
were driven apart by a quarrel.

Their renewed friendship is threatened by Romney's fatal illness. As summer draws to its close, Romney quietly takes his leave ...

... and Hetty returns to teaching, a little sadder, but with her spirit still undaunted.

... the sunshine was as thick and yellow as molten gold; school opened, and we small denizens of the hill farms lived happy days of harmless work and necessary play, closing in nights of peaceful, undisturbed slumber under a roof watched over by autumnal stars.

"*Multiplication is vexation,*
Division is as bad,
The rule of three perplexes me,
And fractions drive me mad."

"*I haven't got as far as fractions yet,*" sighed Sara, "*and I hope I'll be too big to go to school before I do. I hate arithmetic, but I am passionately fond of geography.*"

This particular evening was particularly beautiful. It was cool after a hot day, and wheat fields all about us were ripening to their harvestry, The wind gossiped with the grasses along our way, and over them the buttercups danced, goldenly-glad. Waves of sinuous shadow went over the ripe hayfields, and plundering bees sang a freebooting lilt in wayside gardens.

*Over a valley filled with beech and spruce was a sunset afterglow —
creamy yellow and a hue that was not so much red as the dream of
red ... The air was sweet with the breath of mown hayfields where
swaths of clover had been steeping in the sun. Wild roses grew
pinkly along the fences, and the roadsides were star-dusted with
buttercups.*

October that year gathered up all the spilled sunshine of the summer and clad herself in it as in a garment.

There was something in the fine, elusive air, that recalled beautiful, forgotten things and suggested delicate future hopes. The woods had wrapped fine-woven gossamers about them and the westering hill was crimson and gold.

The days were crisp and mellow, with warm sunshine and a tang of frost in the air, mingled with the woodsy odours of the withering grasses. The hens and turkeys prowled about, pecking at wind-falls ... amid the fallen leaves.

Haylofts are delicious places, with just enough of shadow and soft, uncertain noises to give an agreeable tang of mystery. The swallows flew in and out of their nests above our heads, and wherever a sunbeam fell through a chink the air swarmed with golden dust.

We had a beautiful day for our picnic. November dreamed that it was May. The air was soft and mellow, with pale, aerial mists in the valleys and over the leafless beeches on the western hill. The sere stubble fields brooded in glamour and the sky was pearly blue. The leaves were still thick on the apple trees, though they were russet hued, and the after-growth of grass was richly green, unharmed as yet by the nipping frosts of previous nights. The wind made a sweet, drowsy murmur in the boughs, as of bees among apple blossoms.

"It's just like spring, isn't it?" said Felicity.

The Story Girl shook her head.

"No, not quite. It looks like spring, but it isn't spring. It's as if everything was resting — getting ready to sleep. In spring they're getting ready to grow. Can't you feel the difference?"

"I think it's just like spring," insisted Felicity.

They went back with laughter and raillery over the quiet autumn fields, faintly silvered now by the moon that was rising over the hills.

Late that autumn the children gradually con-
quered their fear of the taciturn Sea-Captain,
who lived in the old lighthouse on the hill.
Ezekiel Crane was his name.

*... a handsome fellow, with the blood of a seafaring
race in his veins.*

She loved the great, restless harbour and the vast, misty sea beyond; she loved the tides, keeping their world-old tryst with the shore, and the gulls, and the croon of the waves, and the call of the winds in the fir woods at noon and even; she loved the moonrises and the sunsets, and the clear, calm nights when the stars seemed to have fallen into the water and to be a little dizzy from such a fall.

It was a diamond winter day ... clear, cold, hard, brilliant. The sharp blue sky shone, the white fields and hills glittered, the fringe of icicles around the eaves of Uncle Alec's house sparkled. Keen was the frost and crisp the snow over our world; and we young fry of the King households were all agog to enjoy life.

It was winter in our orchard of old delights then, — so truly winter that it was hard to believe summer had ever dwelt in it, or that spring would ever return to it. There were no birds to sing the music of the moon; and the path where the apple blossoms had fallen were heaped with less fragrant drifts. But it was a place of wonder on a moonlight night, when the snowy arcades shone like avenues of ivory and crystal and the bare trees cast fairy-like traceries upon them.

The rich winter twilight was purpling over the white
world as they drove down the lane under the over-
arching wild cherry trees that glittered with gemmy
hoar-frost. The snow creaked and crisped under the
runners … Over the trees the sky was a dome of silver,
with a lucent star or two on the slope of the west.

[62]

... we gathered together in the cheer of the red hearth-flame, while outside the wind of a winter twilight sang through fair white valleys brimmed with a reddening sunset, and a faint, serene, silver-cold star glimmered over the willow at the gate.

And it was, as I remember it, a most exquisite night — a white poem, a frosty, starry lyric of light.

Great was the excitement in the houses of King as Christmas drew nigh. The air was simply charged with secrets ... Felicity was in her element, for she and her mother were deep in preparations for the day.

"When I wanted to stone the raisins for the mince-meat she said, no, she would do it herself, because Christmas mince-meat was very particular — as if I couldn't stone raisins right! The airs Felicity puts on about her cooking just make me sick," concluded Cecily wrathfully.

"It's better to know than to imagine," said Felicity.

"Oh, no, it isn't," said the Story Girl quickly. "When you know things you have to go by facts. But when you just dream about things there's nothing to hold you down."

"You're letting the taffy scorch, and that's a fact you'd better go by," said Felicity, sniffing. "Haven't you got a nose?"

All parcels that came in the mail from distant friends were taken charge of by Aunts Janet and Olivia, not to be opened until the great day of the feast itself. How slowly the last week passed! But even watched pots will boil in the fullness of time, and finally Christmas day came ... frost-bitten without, but full of revelry and rose-red mirth within.

The best gift of all that Christmas was the birth
of a baby boy, a new brother for Felicity, Felix
and Cecily, and a baby cousin for Sara.

They were Sara's family now too and she need
never feel lost or lonely again.

Before ... spread the harbour, gray and austere in the
faint light, but afar out the sun was rending asunder
the milk-white mists in which the sea was scarfed,
and under it was a ... glow of sparkling water.
The fir trees on the point moved softly and whispered
together. The whole world sang of spring and
resurrection and life ...